SYDNEY & SIMON
To the MOON!

STORY BY PAUL A. REYNOLDS   ART BY PETER H. REYNOLDS

📖 Charlesbridge

To my son Ben Reynolds who showed us how to "connect the dots" between art and math—which allowed him to blast off to MIT
—P. A. R.

To Helen Obermeyer Simmons, my teacher, my mentor, for supplying the rocket fuel for my journey
—P. H. R.

A note to our readers: Moon phases look different depending on whether you're in the Northern Hemisphere, Southern Hemisphere, or at the equator. Sydney and Simon observe the eight lunar phases from the Northern Hemisphere. While the moon takes about twenty-seven days to orbit Earth, the lunar phase cycle actually takes about twenty-nine days, because, due to the Earth's motion around the sun, it has not finished a full cycle until it reaches the point in its orbit where the sun is in the same position.

Text copyright © 2017 by Paul A. Reynolds
Illustrations copyright © 2017 by Peter H. Reynolds

Published by Charlesbridge
85 Main Street
Watertown, MA 02472
(617) 926-0329
www.charlesbridge.com

Library of Congress Cataloging-in-Publication Data
Reynolds, Paul A., author.
  Sydney & Simon: to the moon!/Paul A. Reynolds; illustrated by Peter H. Reynolds.
    pages cm
  Summary: Twin mice Sydney and Simon compete to create the most interesting project about the Earth's moon for their elementary school, and win the first prize—a chance to meet a real astronaut.
  ISBN 978-1-58089-679-5 (reinforced for library use)
  ISBN 978-1-58089-680-1 (paperback)
  ISBN 978-1-60734-969-3 (ebook)
  ISBN 978-1-60734-970-9 (ebook pdf)
1. Twins—Juvenile fiction. 2. Critical thinking—Juvenile fiction. 3. Brothers and sisters—Juvenile fiction. 4. Science projects—Juvenile fiction. 5. Astronauts—Juvenile fiction. 6. Moon—Juvenile fiction. [1.Twins—Fiction. 2. Mice—Fiction. 3. Brothers and sisters—Fiction. 4. Science projects—Fiction. 5. Schools—Fiction. 6. Moon—Fiction.] I. Reynolds, Peter, 1961– illustrator. II. Title. III. Title: Sydney & Simon. IV. Title: To the moon!
PZ7.R337643Syo 2016
[E]—dc23   2015026877

Printed in China
(hc) 10 9 8 7 6 5 4 3 2 1
(sc) 10 9 8 7 6 5 4 3 2 1

Illustrations created with ink, watercolor wash, water, and tea
Display type set in Chowderhead by Font Diner
Text type set in Schneidler BT by Bitstream Inc.
Color separations by Colourscan Print Co Pte Ltd, Singapore
Printed by 1010 Printing International Limited in Huizhou, Guangdong, China
Production supervision by Brian G. Walker
Reynolds Studio assistance by Julia Anne Young
Designed by Diane M. Earley

Contents

SCIENCE · TECH · ENGINEERING · ARTS · MATH
WONDER FALLS
Elementary
S.T.E.A.M. CHALLENGE
Hometown Hero, Moon Explorer
KRIS KORNFIELD
"Explore the Moon" CONTEST

1

A Stellar Challenge

Wonder Falls Elementary School was having a special STEAM contest: submit the most creative project about Earth's moon, and win first prize.

First prize was the chance to meet astronaut Commander Kris Kornfield!

Sydney and Simon thought this was absolutely out of this world.

"I've got it!" Sydney told her parents. "I have a secret, stellar idea for my moon project."

"*Secret?*" Simon looked concerned. "Well, I'm going to come up with a more stellar-riffic idea. I'm going to be the one to meet Commander Kornfield."

Mrs. Starr added the last wire to her automatic tea-bag-dunker invention.

"The best ideas," she said, "often take time
to brew."

"Not for me," Sydney said, running to the door.
"My *creativi*-tea is ready to pour out!"

"Go ahead," Simon called after his sister. "My
idea will be better!"

"Uh-oh," Mr. Starr chimed in. "Which twin will
win? Let the challenge begin."

2

Sydney's Project Blasts Off

When Sydney reached the Wonder Falls Public Library, she went straight to the Makerspace Lab. She used the computer to design the ultimate entry to the contest: a 3-D moon model. The 3-D printer turned Sydney's digital drawing of the moon into a real, hold-in-your-paws, three-dimensional object. The special printer added thin layers of bioplastic material on top of each other. It took hours to print the entire sphere. But Sydney knew it was worth it.

Later Simon marched up to the apartment roof deck with no idea what to do for his project. Usually he and Sydney loved working as a team. But this time he was on his own.

Above, in the dark night sky, was a big glowing banana. At least that's what the moon looked like.

But Simon knew the moon's big secret! The sun was always shining on half the moon. And as the moon orbited our planet, different amounts of sunlight—sometimes more, sometimes less—could be seen on the half of the moon that faced Earth.

Simon used his Wonder Journal tablet to take photos and search websites.

One site showed all eight moon phases. The first phase was called the new moon—when Simon wouldn't be able to see any light on the moon's surface. He liked to think of it as "The No Moon Phase." The next phase showed the waxing crescent moon. This was when sunlight hit the moon and made it look like a skinny banana from Earth.

"Hey, that's what's in the sky now!" Simon exclaimed. "That's a moon match."

3

Moon-Match Game

Each night Simon continued to observe the sky and play his moon-matching game. Four days after the waxing crescent moon, he could see more sunlight reflecting off the moon. It looked like a half moon. Simon made another match.

"That's the first-quarter moon! Now I've seen two phases." He predicted he would make another match in four more days.

"The next phase is the gibbous moon." He chuckled. "*Gibbous*, that's a funny word! I think I'll name my new pet frog Gibbous."

A few days later Sydney began painting her 3-D printed moon in secret.

"Can I *please* see your project?" Simon asked.

"Sorry, top secret!" Sydney protested.

"Come on," Simon pleaded. "I'm your *twin*. Your best friend. Your wonder bud!"

Sydney didn't budge. She wanted to meet Commander Kris Kornfield more than she wanted anything.

"Well, do you know what waxing gibbous is?" Simon asked.

"Easy. Gibbous is your new frog's name,"
Sydney said.

"Right," Simon groaned. "But a gibbous moon
is when sunlight looks like it's covering most
of the moon's surface. Look out your window.
That's a waxing gibbous moon. Soon it will be
a full moon. Waxing means growing. Waning
means shrinking."

"Simon, you can wax on as much as you like,"
Sydney responded. "But I'm not sharing my idea."

Later that week the full moon was glowing into Sydney's bedroom when Mrs. Starr came in.

"Looks like your project is off to a good start," Sydney's mom told her. "I'm curious about what research you did before creating your moon."

"Mom, I don't have time for research," Sydney explained. "I've seen the moon a thousand times. It's round and bright. And this glow-in-the-dark paint makes my sphere beautiful, just like the actual moon. This will definitely win the contest."

"Ah, but creativity is more than how beautiful something looks," Mrs. Starr said. "Creativity is about shining light on all the pieces of what you're studying, so you can see the bigger picture of how things work."

Sydney wasn't paying attention. She was too busy painting her moon model.

Up on the roof Simon and Mr. Starr were admiring the moon's glow.

"Dad, this full moon is the fifth lunar phase. The moon has orbited to the opposite side of the Earth from where the sun is. From where we are, we can see the entire half of the moon that is covered in sunlight. Another moon match!"

"Wow," said Mr. Starr. "You've learned a lot about the moon's phases and the sun, *son*!"

CLICK
CLICK

Simon grinned. "To win the contest I'm going to share all my research photos, these charts, my moon observations, and the recorded dates and times of each phase."

"Hmmm," said Mr. Starr. "I want you to win, too, Simon, but I wonder if there is a more creative way to present all this information?"

"Dad," Simon said, "I'd love to talk about creativity, but I'm on a mission here. I've really got to get back to my research." And with that, Simon turned to the moon to take another photo.

4

Twinspiration Strikes

One week before the contest, the school was abuzz with excitement. Finn Finster wouldn't tell Sydney and Simon what his project was, but he gave them a clue.

"It's kind of cheesy," he whispered.

"I'm sure it's not that bad," Sydney assured him.

"No, I mean it's *really* cheesy," Finn insisted.

"Sounds delicious!" said Simon.

"Now, class," interrupted Ms. Fractalini. "Let's all head to the STEAM Studio."

Ms. Fractalini's STEAM Studio was where she encouraged her students to use Science, Technology, Engineering, Arts, and Math to imagine new discoveries and to see the creative connections among all subjects.

"Today," Ms. Fractalini revealed, "we will get to know a STEAM thinker who lived about four hundred years ago. His name was Galileo, and he kept his eye on the sky."

Galileo had been a scientist, engineer, mathematician, astronomer, *and* artist.

"Galileo was one cool dude," Finn said. "Way back in the 1600s, he discovered that Jupiter had four moons!"

"That's right, Finn," Ms. Fractalini said. "Galileo's work might give you all some final inspiration for the Explore the Moon contest."

Sydney searched for more information on the computer. "Fab-awesome! Look at Galileo's watercolor paintings of Earth's moon."

"I love those," Ms. Fractalini said. "They are gorgeous, but they are also accurate. Galileo took the time to observe the moon and use his artistic talent to take note of what he was seeing and learning."

"This is really smart art," Sydney thought. She
realized that she hadn't studied the moon very
closely before she rushed into designing and then
fabricating it on the 3-D printer.

25

"How could Galileo see all that detail on the surface of the moon?" Simon asked.

"Galileo built one of the first telescopes to view the moon," Finn answered.

"Wow! He painted the moon *and* invented things?" Simon said. "He really used STEAM thinking to go above and beyond."

Simon was worried. Maybe his dad was right after all. Presenting photos and charts of his moon research didn't sound so imaginative now.

That's when a flash of twinspiration hit.

5

Twinergy to the Rescue

That night Simon called an official Starr twin meeting. Sydney snacked on cheese balls during her brother's twinspirational talk.

"Syd," he began, "today made me realize that we need each other."

Sydney nibbled another cheese ball. She paused for a moment. Today's visit to the STEAM Studio *had* made her curious about the moon's phases. Maybe Simon's observations could help her after all.

"Well, I'm thinking my project could use some of your research," she admitted.

"And knowing how good your imagination is, I could use some of your creativity," Simon said.

Sydney revealed her glow-in-the-dark 3-D moon to Simon at last. She warned him, "It's nice to look at, but it won't help people learn much about the moon."

Simon brought out his charts and photos. "Well, I have all these observations about the phases of the moon," he said. "But it's not a very creative way to show what I know."

That's when they gave each other an *are-you-thinking-what-I'm-thinking?* super-twin glance.

"If we work together," said Simon, "we'll fuel
our moon mission project with . . ."

"TWINERGY!" they said together.

They ran up to the roof deck filled with
thoughts of a new double-stellar moon project.

Simon pointed up. "Sydney, this moon phase is the waning gibbous. Just a few days ago we saw the full moon. Now, as the moon keeps orbiting Earth, the amount of sunlight that we can see reflected on the lunar surface is waning, or shrinking."

Sydney stood on tiptoe and looked really hard.

"I just wish we could see the surface of the moon better," she said. "Hey, if Galileo could make a telescope, why can't we?"

"That's it! Let's build our own TeleTwin Telescope," Simon said. "We'll be able to record more details before making a new project together."

Sydney loved that idea. *"Twintastic!"*

The twins hunted for all the parts they needed to build a telescope.

After testing and improving their design, they were ready to take a closer look at the moon.

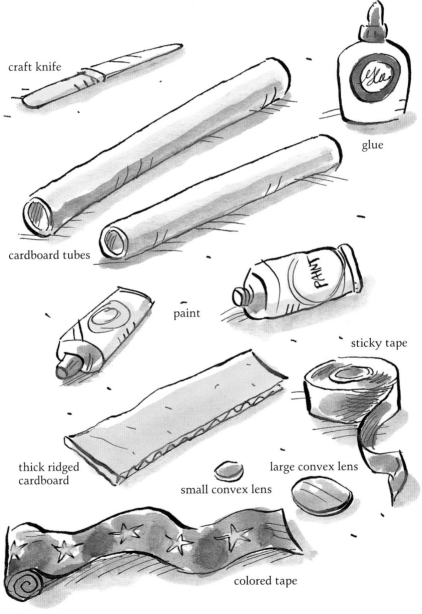

craft knife

glue

cardboard tubes

paint

sticky tape

thick ridged cardboard

small convex lens

large convex lens

colored tape

A few nights after, they could see actual craters on the lunar surface. Sydney also observed sunlight reflecting off the left side of the moon. She checked Simon's chart.

"I made a moon match! That's the last-quarter moon phase!" she noted.

Simon was proud of their telescope, too. He peered through it next and used his tablet to sketch what he saw.

With their telescope, the twins continued to observe the moon over the next week until they spotted the final lunar phase: the waning crescent. It looked like another skinny banana!

Thanks to Simon's photos and charts, Sydney now knew each phase like the back of her paw. And she introduced Simon to the library's 3-D printer.

Together they used their research and drawings to fabricate and paint a 3-D moon puzzle. Each piece was one of the eight moon phases, complete with craters!

The night before the contest, getting their project ready for the big day made the twins hungry.

"How about quiche for dinner?" asked Mrs. Starr.

"Oh, but I wanted cheesy pasta with broccoli," said Mr. Starr.

"Sometimes," Simon said, "it's best to blend different ideas together. Right, Syd?"

"Precisely," agreed Sydney. And with that, the Starr family made a cheesy-broccoli-pasta-quiche dinner. This made *everybody* happy.

6

And the Winner Is...

Finally it was the day to present their finished projects. Sydney and Simon were nervous. Were they the only students who decided to work together? With their 3-D-printed moon-phase puzzle and homemade telescope, they bravely walked into the STEAM Studio.

STEAM-powered collaboration was everywhere!

One group had built a small model house made entirely with toothpicks, which they imagined constructing on the moon one day.

Jed Moxley had sculpted a moon crater big enough to crawl in, and Markesha Minza recited a poem she had written about rare blue moons.

Finn Finster and Nina Fixley showed off a hanging mobile of the moon, Earth, and sun made entirely of cheese. And everyone admired the giant cardboard rocket ship Blake Feldspar made. It was inspired by a real spacecraft.

Sydney and Simon were amazed. Choosing a winner would not be easy.

"I would love-love-love to meet Commander Kornfield, but I won't even mind if we don't win."

"*Really?*" Simon asked.

"Really," Sydney replied. "Winning would be awesome. But *twinning* is even better."

Simon agreed. "Working together reminded us that collaboration can fuel fab creations!"

"All right, students, time to quiet down," Ms. Fractalini interrupted. "Congratulations to everyone on your wonder-filled, wonderful projects! I will now announce the winner of the most creative STEAM-inspired project about Earth's moon."

For good luck Simon crossed his tail with Sydney's.

"And . . . the winner is . . . " Ms. Fractalini paused.

". . . all of you!" Ms. Fractalini said. "You will *all* get to meet Commander Kris Kornfield!"

In walked their astronaut hero.

The students gasped. Everyone cheered.

When Commander Kornfield reached Sydney and Simon, she inspected their work. "This is definitely an arts-and-smarts project! Galileo would have been proud of your telescope, and your puzzle will teach and inspire future astronauts."

The twins exchanged glances. Together they gave their 3-D puzzle to Commander Kornfield as a gift.

The astronaut was awestruck. "Thank you both. Your kindness and creativity will take you really far."

"Thanks, Commander," Simon said. "We hope that someday they'll take us to the *real* moon . . ."

". . . and beyond!" Sydney added.

Glossary

3-D printer—a machine that allows layers of material to form three-dimensional solid objects under the control of a computer

art—something (such as a painting, drawing, song, or sculpture) that is created with imagination, is beautiful, or shows important ideas or feelings

astronaut—a person who travels into outer space in a spacecraft

astronomer—a person who studies the planets, stars, and outer space

blue moon—a rare second full moon in a calendar month

creativity—the skill to think of new ideas or make new things

engineering—the work of creating and designing structures or complex machines (such as bridges or telescopes) by engineers (people who apply science and math to make systems, machines, or products)

fabricate—to construct an object from prepared materials

first-quarter moon—the third phase of the moon, which occurs when the right half of the moon is lit by the sun, as seen from Earth

full moon—the fifth phase of the moon, which occurs when the moon is completely illuminated, as seen from Earth

Galileo Galilei—an Italian astronomer, engineer, philosopher, and mathematician who was important to the scientific revolution between the late 1500s and early 1600s

invention—an original device, machine, or method created by someone (the inventor)

lab—a room with special equipment for doing experiments, science, or other test-related work

last-quarter moon—the seventh phase of the moon, which occurs when the left half of the moon is lit by the sun on its way back to the new moon phase, as seen from Earth

lunar—of or relating to the moon

math—the science of numbers, shapes, and quantities and the relations among them

mobile—a work of art that is hung from above and has materials attached to it that move easily in the air

moon crater—a round hole on the surface of the moon formed by impact

moon phase—the shape of the illuminated or sunlit portion of the moon as seen by people on Earth

new moon—the first phase of the moon, when the moon's shadow inhibits viewers from Earth from seeing the sun's reflection off the moon's surface

observe—to watch or listen carefully

orbit—to travel completely around something (such as Earth) in a circular path

research—careful study that is done to collect new information about something

science—information about or the study of the natural world based on facts learned through observations and experiments

tablet—a mobile computer with a touchscreen display that usually comes equipped with a camera and microphone

technology—the use of science in industry or engineering to help solve problems or invent useful things; a machine or piece of equipment that is made by technology, such as a computer tablet

telescope—a long, tube-shaped device that you look through in order to make things that are far away appear closer

twinergy—Sydney and Simon's joint enthusiasm and effort

twinspiration—a great idea powered by Sydney and Simon's experience as twins

waning crescent moon—the eighth phase of the moon, when a small portion of the left side of the moon is lit by the sun, and the moon is decreasing in illumination

waning gibbous moon—the sixth phase of the moon, when nearly the entire left side of the moon is lit by the sun, and the moon is decreasing in illumination

waxing crescent moon—the second phase of the moon, when a small portion of the right side of the moon is lit by the sun, and the moon is increasing in illumination, as seen from Earth

waxing gibbous moon—the fourth phase of the moon, when nearly the entire right side of the moon is lit by the sun, and the moon is increasing in illumination

website—a place on the internet or World Wide Web that contains information about an organization, person, group, or subject

Wonder Journal—Sydney and Simon's physical or electronic books where they write down thoughts and ideas

Making Stellar STEAM Discoveries . . . Together!

Dear Readers,

Did you know that we are twins, just like Sydney and Simon? When we were growing up, we were doubly curious about everything—including the stars, space, and the moon. We loved playing, creating, and learning together.

We still remember when we were eight years old and watched the first human walking on the moon. It seemed almost impossible! But we began to understand that when people use their smarts and creativity, they can do the most amazing things.

Sydney and Simon learn a lot about the moon in this latest adventure. But the twins' most important discovery is when they realize how working *together* can improve everyone's learning journey. And when collaboration includes STEAM thinking, well, get ready to rocket even farther on your learning adventures!

STEAM stands for Science, Technology, Engineering, Arts, and Math. Adding the "A" for "Arts" to "STEM" means using *imagination* and *creativity* to problem-solve and make new discoveries across subjects. Who knows—maybe you'll use those arts and smarts to explore outer space one day!

Try using STEAM thinking to collaborate with *your* best friend. Can you use your combined creativity to invent a spaceship—one that you could travel in to the edge of the Milky Way galaxy? If you worked together to design a house or school on the moon, what would it look like? Can you team up to invent a game to play on the International Space Station—where microgravity is at work? How many ways can art help you to better understand the world—and universe—around you?

When you use your STEAM thinking and work together with others to imagine, create, discover, and learn—please let us know. We'd love to hear and see what you've done!

Wishing you stellar STEAM adventures ahead,

PAUL & PETER

48